Sara Galadari is an Emirati best-selling author, having written numerous books for children and young adults. Bitten by a bookworm as a young child, she developed an unquenchable thirst for consuming every book she could get her hands on.

Born and raised in Dubai, United Arab Emirates, she spent her youth visiting libraries and checking out dozens of books at a time (taking advantage of her brothers' library cards to cheat the system and check out even more books for the week). After taking an interest in how language can shape meaning across culture, society, media, and cognitive processes, she went on to get her BA and MSc in Communication.

Sara draws from her education to write stories that touch on pivotal topics, with the hopes of shaping bright minds to build a better tomorrow.

For my father, whose humour always struck me as a little odd.
For my mother, who helped me begin my journey as a writer.

Sara Galadari

THE PIGEON CHRONICLES

AUSTIN MACAULEY PUBLISHERS™
LONDON • CAMBRIDGE • NEW YORK • SHARJAH

ISBN – 9789948799610 – (Paperback)
ISBN – 9789948799627 – (E-Book)

Application Number: MC-10-01-7222766
Age Classification: E

Printer Name: iPrint Global Ltd
Printer Address: Witchford, England

First Published 2023
AUSTIN MACAULEY PUBLISHERS FZE
Sharjah Publishing City
P.O Box [519201]
Sharjah, UAE
www.austinmacauley.ae
+971 655 95 202

Table of Contents

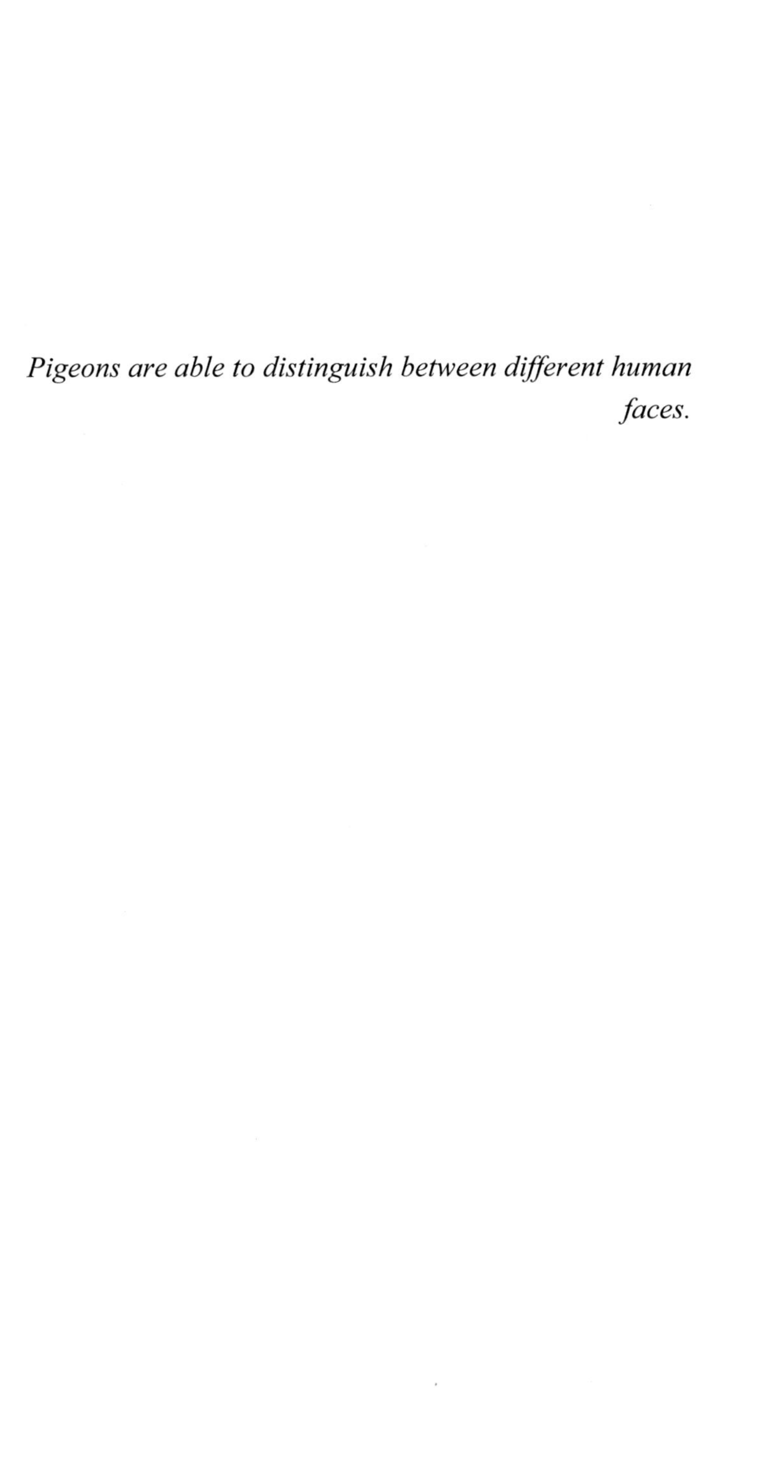

Pigeons are able to distinguish between different human faces.

How It All Began

Bobby giggled, his chubby feet pounding across the pavement as he chased the little pigeon that was perched on the curb side. He kneeled down onto his haunches and waved the stick he was carrying in the air. "I'm gonna get you," he said to the little pigeon, his little figure casting a shadow over it. The pigeon seemed to ignore the little boy, cocking its head to the side before pecking repeatedly at the ground.

"I said," Bobby repeated as he crawled closer to the pigeon, his stick tightly clutched in a curled-up fist. "I'm gonna GET YOU," he accidentally poked the pigeon with the stick as he lunged forwards. He let out a high-pitched squeal as the pigeon fluttered its wings in slight panic at the unfamiliar object that was currently prodding it in the chest. A few feathers came floating down from the bird, and Bobby's squeals turned into ones of delight as he began grabbing at them.

"Ooh! I can use these for my art project!" Bobby exclaimed as he piled the feathers neatly into a corner. He stood up, wobbling slightly as he put a hand to his chin thoughtfully. "I think I need more." He turned his head slowly and eyed the pigeon, smirking. The pigeon fluffed up its wings and drew its head further out, trying to make itself seem more threatening to the little boy. All Bobby saw, however, was more feathers.

"Bobby! Leave that poor bird alone!"

Bobby snapped his head around towards the direction of a slender woman standing in the doorway of a house, a few feet away from where he was.

"But, Sally! I want its feathers for my art project!" Bobby yelled back at his sister, his voice ending with a whine.

"Bobby Brooks. You leave that poor creature alone. Right now. Besides, it's time for your bath." Bobby winced as he heard his full name being used. He only heard his full name when he was going to be in trouble. He wondered briefly why that was.

"But I don't wanna take a bath!"

"Bobby! Now!"

"Fine," he huffed, unwillingly putting his stick down. He padded back to his front yard, scowling at his big sister.

"You shouldn't be cruel to animals," she berated him, putting her hands on her hips. "Besides, don't you know that pigeons never forget a face?"

"No," Bobby muttered, shifting uncomfortably under her gaze. How stupid was she? Pigeons can't remember anything! Why, he was poking at the same pigeon yesterday, and it didn't seem to remember him at all today!

"Well, they don't. And if you're not careful, you're going to have a very angry flock of pigeons attacking a little five-year-old boy."

"I'm five and *a half*," Bobby corrected, sticking his tongue out at her. Sally rolled her eyes.

"Whatever. Go take your bath now. I need to finish getting ready to meet my friends."

"But I don't wanna take a bath," Bobby whined, stamping his little foot on the ground.

He didn't seem to notice the pigeon hopping over and examining its lost feathers that were piled up by the curb as Bobby argued with his sister. Finally, he begrudgingly trotted back into the house, muttering about how silly everything was. His sister, the pigeon, the stick…

Besides, what did Sally know, anyway? She was only seventeen. The pigeon was surely going to forget him.

He climbed the stairs up to his room and poked at the small vial of glitter that was perched precariously on his little desk. He grumbled, annoyed, as he uncorked the vial and began fiddling with its contents. Whatever was he to do now? He didn't want to take a bath yet…

He sighed, walking over to his window and peering outside. It was getting dark. He wasn't allowed to play outside once it got dark. He sighed again, poking a tiny finger at the glass while resting his head on his palm.

Clink. Clink.

Bobby jumped back in surprise as something began clinking onto the window in response.

It was the pigeon! Looking back at his door mischievously to make sure no one was watching him, he quietly slid his window open and let the bird flutter inside. It cocked its head at the boy before hopping onto his table.

"Hello, little pigeon," Bobby cooed at the bird. He jerked back as the pigeon fluffed up its wings and cooed back at him. "I'm bored, pigeon! What do I—" Bobby stopped in midsentence as his eyes laid on the vial of glitter. He grinned cheekily, clutching the vial and unscrewing the lid. He reached out and grabbed a bottle of Elmer's glue. The pigeon's eyes widened slightly as it began to inch backwards.

Unfortunately for the pigeon, Bobby was too quick for it to do anything but flap its wings in alarm. He raised the bottle of glue high above the bird and squeezed, watching the stream of glue slowly oozing out and dribbling across its feathers. He then sprinkled the glitter onto the pigeon, careful not to make a mess on the table (his mother usually berated him for doing so). The pigeon, too stunned to do anything, stood frozen in its spot.

Bobby took a few steps back and admired his handiwork. The pigeon was an angry, sticky, gluey, glittery mess. It glared at Bobby as he happily clapped his hands, quite pleased with himself.

How could this tiny human being be so… *evil*? The pigeon glowered at the child, trying to shake off the glitter from its wings before it got stuck there permanently. It eyed the window for a moment. It was still cracked open.

Maybe it could make a quick escape… It was only a few feet away, after all…

"Where are you going, Pigeon?" Bobby demanded, noticing the pigeon inching towards the windowsill. It was so close to freedom… "You forgot your eyes!"

The pigeon, all too familiar with human-speech, froze in its place. Eyes? Whatever did this little human mean? Was he going to pull out its eyes?

Its question was soon answered. It felt some pressure onto its back, and turned its head in horror to see some more glue dripping down its beautiful, shiny coat of feathers. It then felt a shower of googly-eyes rain down onto its back. Finally, a pair of pipe cleaners, fashioned as sparkly antennas, was delicately placed on its head.

"There you go," chirped Bobby happily. "Now you look so pretty!"

The pigeon turned and faced its reflection in the window. Patches of multi-coloured glitter sparkled across its body, and the disproportionate amount of glue that Bobby had poured onto it had mixed with its feathers to form some kind of matted paste. Its back was covered in a shell of googly-eyes that stared eerily back at him, and the antennas that balanced on its head set off the entire look.

Which looked far, *far* from pretty.

It turned around and stared dangerously at Bobby, whose laughs had died down into a nervous chuckle. He finally fell silent as the pigeon let out an ominous "croo."

The pigeon flapped its wings, spraying Bobby with a few droplets of glittery glue as it made its way towards the window.

"Hey! What's that white thing you left on my table?" Bobby demanded angrily. He neared the table and bent down, sniffing deeply. "Ewwww! You pooped on my table!"

The pigeon let out another indignant "croo," turning its head back at Bobby as it began to fly away.

"Hey! Come back here! How am I going to explain this?" Bobby yelled after the bird as it dashed away for its escape.

Little did that tiny human know that this would not be the last time he would encounter its excrements. Flapping its wings with its silent vow, it flew, disappearing into the glowing light of the sunset.

"Bobby! Have you taken your bath yet?"

Bobby shrank back from the window and hurriedly ran towards the bathroom at the sound of Sally's question.

"No! I'm not taking a bath!" he called out to her, getting ready to make a dash for it himself.

"Bobby, you get your tiny butt in the bathroom before I haul you in there myself... What is that on your shoulder?"

Bobby stopped in his tracks and pulled at his sleeve, examining it closely. It looked like glue.

He narrowed his eyes at it, a familiar scent wafting towards his nostrils. Realizing what it was, he wrinkled his nose in disgust.

"IT'S BIRD POOP!" he shrieked, suddenly running towards his sister in a panic. "I HAVE BIRD POOP ON ME!"

"EW! GET AWAY FROM ME!" Sally shrieked back, hastily moving away from her little brother as he hurtled past her. "Go into the bathroom and take your bath, now!"

"NEVER! I'LL NEVER GET INTO THE BATHROOM!"

Sally threw her hands up in the air, at a loss. "You have BIRD POOP on you! BIRD POOP, BOBBY!"

"I'M STILL CLEAN! I'LL JUST CHANGE MY SHIRT!" he yelled at her, still running around. He pulled his little T-shirt over his head and threw it behind him.

Unfortunately, it fell right onto Sally's head.

"That is IT," Sally screamed, horrified at the thought of bird faeces touching her hair. She began to chase after her little brother, determined to get him into his bath. Catching up to him, she wrapped her hands around his legs and began to drag him towards the direction of the bathroom.

"Let me go!" yelled Bobby, kicking at his sister.

"No!" she yelled back at him, tugging at his legs. He grasped onto one of the pillars of the staircase, holding on for dear life.

"LET GO OF THE STAIRCASE!"

"NEVER! I'LL NEVER LET GO!"

"LET GO!"

"OVER MY DEAD BODY!"

"THEN I GUESS YOU LEAVE ME NO CHOICE BUT TO DRAG YOUR DEAD BODY TO THE BATH!"

"YOU CAN'T DO THAT! THAT MEANS YOU'D KILL ME!"

"THAT'S EXACTLY WHAT I MEAN!"

"YOU CAN'T DO THAT! YOU'LL GO TO JAIL FOR BEING A MURDERER!"

"SO WHAT? AT LEAST YOU'LL BE A CLEAN, DEAD, LITTLE BOY!" Sally shouted, completely losing her temper. Bobby finally let go of the staircase, questioning his sister's sanity and slightly fearing for his own safety.

"HA HA!" Sally whooped triumphantly. She picked him up and threw him over her shoulder, making her way towards the bathroom.

"Put me down, I'll go take my stupid bath!" Bobby grumbled, defeated.

"Oh, no. I'm not falling for that," said Sally, scoffing. She opened the door to the bathroom and set him down onto the floor.

"I can do the rest myself," Bobby insisted, folding his arms as he watched his sister turn the tap on.

She eyed him, suspicious. "Really!" Bobby insisted.

"Alright," she sighed. "Get in the bath. And be quick! I have to go get ready *again* for my date tonight." She walked out of the bathroom and closed the door behind her. Bobby climbed into the tub, fiddling with the soap as he frothed the water about. He quite enjoyed bubble baths, despite the fuss he made earlier.

After a while of lounging about in the bathtub with his toy robots and rubber ducky, Bobby began to grow bored. He glanced at the small window at the side.

"It's getting a little too hot in here," Bobby mused aloud, fanning away the steam rising from the bathwater. He padded out of the bathtub, dripping water everywhere, as he made his way towards the window. He stood on his tiptoes and pushed against the glass, smiling as a small breeze wafted in.

Suddenly, a small dark figure darted into the corner of his vision. Frowning, he shifted his gaze in its direction, but it seemed to have disappeared. Shrugging, he went back into the bath and began playing with his toys.

While in the middle of making his toy airplane plunge into the water, he heard a small scratching sound.

"Who's there?" he called out uncertainly.

Scratch. Scratch.

"H-hello?" he gulped, his mind jumping to monsters and gargoyles. "Sally!" he cried. "SALLY!"

He froze, his eyes drawn to the small figure that was slowly poking its head into the window. He felt his skin break out in a cold sweat, imagining whatever creature that was going to crawl its way in was going to do to him, when…

"Oh," Bobby sighed. "Pigeon!" He clambered out of the bathtub once more and walked over to the bird, the pipe cleaners wavering slightly on its head as it cocked its head to the side. "Sally was right! Pigeons really don't forget faces! You *do* remember me!" Bobby squealed happily.

"Croo," the bird fluffed its feathers. With that, it hopped onto Bobby's head and settled into his hair. "Ow, your feet are digging into my head," he complained, feeling the bird's claws curling around clumps of his hair. He waved his hands on top of his head, shooing the bird away.

The pigeon flapped its wings as it settled onto the windowsill, the googly eyes that were still glued onto its back boring holes into Bobby.

"Is everything alright?" Sally poked her head into the bathroom. "Why is the window open—what is that on your head?" she asked in disbelief.

"What do you mean? There's nothing on my—" Bobby stopped talking as he faced his reflection in the mirror. There, sitting on his head, was a large, white splat.

Oh, yes… That little human should have listened to his sister… Pigeons never forget faces.

And this pigeon was never going to forget Bobby's face.

"Croo."

Pigeon droppings are considered a nuisance nowadays. However, centuries ago, pigeon droppings were considered quite valuable, and were even protected by guards.

Ice Cream

"Higher! Push me higher!"

Bobby grinned as he kicked his legs in the air, clutching onto the chains of his swing. Behind him, Sally was reluctantly pushing her little brother, begrudgingly muttering about having to babysit him *again*. He was eight years old now, *why* did she have to watch him at the playground?

Seriously, this boy was ruining her social life.

Feeling the tell-tale rhythm of her phone vibrating in her pocket, she shooed Bobby away from the swings so that she could text in peace.

"But Sally!" Bobby whined. "I'm not done with the swings!"

"Hmm?" She was focused entirely on her phone, her fingers flying over the keyboard.

"Sally!"

"Bobby, stop being so annoying. Go play and make some new friends," she huffed, turning her attention away from her tiny screen and to her brother.

"Fine," he muttered, moodily shuffling his feet in the sand that spanned out across the playground. He made his way over to the slides and stood there, spying on the children who were playing with each other. They all seemed to know each other already and have their own little circle of friends. They all never wanted to play with him, sensing something odd about Bobby.

He sighed.

Bobby sat down on the slide and pushed himself down, suppressing a delighted squeal as he slid down. As he neared the end of the slide, he gained too much momentum and flew off the end, pummelling straight into a hard object.

Thud.

"Ow! That hurt!"

Bobby scrambled off of the object, which turned out to be a little girl, and straightened himself up before reaching a hand down to help her up.

"I'm sorry," he said. "I was sliding down way too fast and I couldn't stop myself. Besides! Didn't anyone ever tell you not to stand in front of a slide before?" he berated, sounding slightly like his big sister when she was telling him off for doing something silly.

"You're mean," the girl said in response, turning her nose up at him as she dusted her skirt off. With that, she flipped her little ponytails behind her and stomped away.

Bobby was dumbfounded.

What had he done wrong? All he had done was help her up after *she* was stupidly standing in front of the slide. It wasn't his fault. It was an accident. He wasn't mean.

She was mean.

Oh, he'd show her what mean was like.

He stormed over to her and pulled at her pigtails before running away and hiding behind one of the poles in the jungle gym, chuckling to himself. She'd never figure out who did it. He was way too fast for her.

His chuckles died down as he felt something poke his shoulder. He turned around and saw the girl standing before him, furious, her arms folded across her chest.

"What was that for?" she demanded.

"You called me mean!" Bobby retaliated.

"You pushed me down in front of the slide!"

"Well *you* were standing in front of the slide!"

The girl took a deep breath in. "Alright, we were both wrong." She stuck a hand out to him. "We should call a truce." Bobby looked down at her hand in confusion.

"Er- what are you doing?"

"You have to shake my hand, silly," she said, as if it was the most obvious thing in the world. She grabbed his sweaty hand and shook it, demonstrating what she meant. "Now that we shook hands, we have officially declared a truce," she smiled. "I'm Emily. What's your name?"

"Bobby," he introduced himself shyly.

"Well, Bobby. It's very nice to meet you. We should be friends!" she declared. "It'll be great, you can come over to my tea parties and play dolls with me and—"

"What? Ewww, no! Those stuff are for *girls*," said Bobby disdainfully.

"Well, *I* like to play tea party," Emily folded her arms firmly.

"Well, *I* don't like playing tea party," he huffed.

"Okay. What do you like to do?" she asked. Bobby shrugged. "I dunno. I like to jump off of stuff…"

"I think tea parties are fun. You should come over and play with me!" Emily insisted, smiling at him. He noticed a tooth missing from her smile, and ran his tongue over his own gums, feeling the loose tooth shaking in its socket.

"How about we find something we both like to do?" he said. He suddenly heard a low, tinkling sound.

That sounded like…

He turned his head around and grinned, hearing the tinkling grow louder and louder.

"The ice-cream truck is here!" he jumped up and down ecstatically. Emily joined in with his jumping.

"I think we found something that we both like," said Emily in between jumps.

"Let's go get some!" Bobby exclaimed, nodding along with her. He ran over to Sally and sneakily slipped a bill out of her wallet from her purse. She didn't seem to notice, seeing as she had gotten into a frantic texting war with someone.

Grinning mischievously to himself, he ran back over to Emily and opened up the bill. Their jaws both simultaneously dropped as they realized they had a crisp hundred-dollar bill in their hands.

"Do you know how many ice cream bars we could buy with a hundred dollars?" Bobby said, his eyes growing as round as dinner plates.

"We could live on ice cream for the rest of our lives," murmured Emily dreamily.

Bobby was suddenly made aware of the tinkling sound of the ice cream truck slowly fading away. He took off after it, Emily dashing behind him.

"Wait! Wait for us!" he cried, clutching the money in his hand as he chased after the truck. Eventually, the old ice cream truck driver noticed the two children and slowed down the vehicle.

"Why hello there, young man. What can I do for you?"

"I'd like all the ice cream that this can buy," Bobby beamed as he handed the man the one-hundred-dollar bill. The man's eyebrows raised slightly before quickly pocketing the money and eyeing Bobby doubtfully.

"Where did you get this from?" he asked, narrowing his eyes at the two children.

"Uhh, it's mine!" said Bobby quickly. Bobby and Emily grinned innocently up at him.

The man raised an eyebrow at him, his suspicion growing.

"These darned spoiled kids these days…" the man muttered to himself as he got out of the truck. "Alright, you two will have cleaned me out. Help yourselves to the ice cream in the back," he told the children, popping the back of the trunk open.

A vague reminder echoed through his head as he thought about getting into the truck. The man was a stranger, after all… What was it that his mother always told him? Never get into a stranger's car.

But this man had ice cream!

Bobby was about to step into the truck when a shriek stopped him in his path.

"Bobby! What are you *doing*?!" Sally stormed over to him, her hands on both of her hips as she glared at him. "Shame on you," she huffed at the man before hauling Bobby away, ignoring his cries for ice cream.

"Were you about to get into that man's truck? What if he had taken you? Do you have any idea how much trouble I'd get into?" she lectured him, waving a finger at his face.

"But I already paid the man…"

"Oh, alright. Let me go get some ice cream for you and, uh, what's your name?" she asked Emily, noticing the little girl standing next to Bobby.

"Emily," she chirped.

"Right." Sally rolled her eyes and walked over to the ice cream truck. Bobby watched as she opened her wallet, her eyes pop wide open in panic as she realized that it was empty. She frantically began to search through every pocket of her purse.

"It has to be here somewhere," she said to herself, sounding more and more flustered. Bobby opened his mouth, about to confess to what he did, but quickly reconsidered when she let out a small growl. She dropped down to her knees and quickly began searching through the leaves that littered the roads.

He heard a small rustling in the trees above him, and he lifted his head to see two pigeons perched on the branches above.

One of them had a vaguely familiar sparkle to its coat of feathers…

"I have to get going, lady," the ice cream truck driver said hurriedly, eager to take off with his hundred dollars.

Bobby glared at the truck driver. How dare he try and take off with the money without giving him the ice cream? He sighed.

He knew what had to be done.

"Sally, I took the money from your wallet and paid the ice cream man," he admitted, shamefully looking down at the floor.

Sally, still on all fours frantically searching among the leaves, froze at her little brother's confession.

"You *what?!*" she shrieked. "That's my entire pay check! You were about to spend my entire pay check on *ice cream?* And without telling me? Oh, I could just kill you right now!" she yelled, her eyes glinting with rage.

She was interrupted by the sound of the ice cream truck's tinkling as the ice cream truck driver tried to make his getaway.

"And you!" she stormed towards him. "Give me my money back!"

The driver huffed moodily, his plans of keeping the hundred dollars ruined by the little boy.

While Sally and the ice cream truck driver were arguing over the money, Bobby nudged Emily at the back of the ice cream truck.

It was open.

The ice cream was just sitting there, practically begging to be eaten.

Stealing was wrong, however, Bobby mused. He looked up at the ice cream truck driver, deep in thought.

"He deserves to be punished for trying to cheat my sister!" he whispered to Emily. She nodded in agreement.

Emily glanced at the two arguing adults. Neither of them seemed to be paying any attention to them…

Grinning mischievously at each other, Bobby and Emily snuck into the back of the ice cream truck and grabbed a few cones each. They raced away with their stolen frozen treats, eager to gobble them up before they were caught by anyone.

"Let's hide over here," Emily pointed behind a large tree. They huddled at the base of its trunk, giggling.

Bobby began unwrapping his ice cream cone, his mouth watering as he greedily eyed the smooth, creamy vanilla ice cream with chocolate sprinkles. He was just about to take a bite from it when a shadow fell over him. He looked up just in time to see two small objects coming directly at him from the sky. He yelled and ducked, narrowly avoiding contact with them.

"What are those?" Emily asked, watching the object turn around in the sky and fly back towards them.

"I don't know! Duck!" Bobby wailed. They dodged the aerial attack once more, except this time with a terrible casualty. Bobby watched in dismay as his ice cream slid off of the cone and fell with a splat onto the side of the pavement.

"NOOOOO," Bobby cried as he fell to his knees, mourning at the loss of his uneaten ice cream. He stared at the small puddle on the pavement that his ice cream was turning into.

"It's alright, it's just ice cream," said Emily, taking a large bite out of her own ice cream as she consoled her new friend. Bobby was just about to snarkily reply when her own ice cream slid off of its cone, joining Bobby's ice cream.

They both stared at the ice cream that was slowly melting into a creamy puddle. She burst into tears.

"I have an idea!" said Bobby, uneasily staring at his bawling friend. "Quick! Before it all melts away! We can eat the parts that hasn't touched the pavement yet!" he said, getting down on all fours and getting ready to salvage the remaining ice cream.

Just as he was nearing his first bite of the ice cream, he heard a small *plop*, followed by Emily's shriek of "Ewwww!"

Bobby pulled back and examined the ice cream. It couldn't be.

Could it?

Bobby looked up at the sky and saw the two pigeons circling him. Seeming to notice the boy's glare, they flapped their wings and settled onto the ground beside him.

"Shoo! Go away, pigeons!" Bobby cried, waving his arms at the two pesky creatures.

"Croo."

"GO AWAY! YOU POOPED ON MY ICE CREAM, YOU HORRIBLE BIRDS!" Bobby cried through tears. "SHOO!" The pigeons just stared at him.

"You could have pooped anywhere else," Bobby sobbed, not noticing Emily slowly backing away. "Why did you have to poop on my ice cream? You could have done it *anywhere* else!"

With that, the pigeons flapped their wings, settled onto either side of Bobby's shoulders for a moment, and then flew away.

Bobby sighed sadly before making his way back to Emily.

"You have bird poop on your shirt!" Emily squealed, pointing at the spots where the pigeons had just been. Bobby jumped and turned his head to examine his shoulders. Sure enough, there were two large, gooey, white splotches on his shoulder. He reached down and pulled his shirt over his head.

"It's okay! I'm still clean! I'll just change my shirt!" he yelled reassuringly.

Emily, however, was far from being reassured.

Sally looked up from her phone as she heard a little girl's scream. Next to Bobby, she saw the little girl and what was her name again? Emily? Emma? Something or the other—with Bobby's shirt draped over her head as she ran around in circles, sounding panicked.

That was strange. Why did this seem vaguely familiar to her?

She saw two pigeons calmly perched on a tree near the two children observing the chaotic scene unfolding before them.

"Oh no," Sally said to herself in disbelief. "Not again."

Do the Math

"Alright, class. You may begin your test," Mr. Hall's voice droned monotonously. Bobby grumbled, tapping the back of his pencil onto his test as he glared at the math problems staring back at him.

Oh, how he hated long division.

He glanced at the first few problems and decided that he didn't know how to solve them, so he turned to the next row of problems. He remembered what his teacher had once told him when it came to tests: If you're unsure of how to answer the question, skip it, move on to the next one, and then come back to it later. He sighed.

What was he supposed to do if he didn't know how to solve *any* of the problems?

He continued tapping his pencil against his notebook as he contemplated the numbers.

Tap. Tap. Tap.

How on earth was figuring out the solution to 543 ÷ 7 ever going to be useful to him? Why were they even learning long division? Why did the third grade have to be so hard?

He tapped his pencil against the desk in frustration.

Tap. Tap. Tap.

He tried to peer at his classmate's test beside him, but froze as he heard Mr. Hall clear his throat and glare sternly at him.

"Eyes on your own paper, Mr. Brooks," Mr. Hall boomed. Bobby muttered angrily to himself, rubbing his chin with the back of his pencil.

He was staring so hard at the math equation, as if it were going to jump up out of the page and present the solution to him.

He stared at the 7. No, he glared at it. Oh, how he hated numbers.

Tap. Tap. Tap.

"Could you knock it off?" hissed Emily from behind him. "You're ruining my concentration."

Bobby turned to glare at Emily instead. He peeked at her paper and saw that she was on the last question already.

How did she get there so fast?

It wasn't fair.

It wasn't fair at all.

He knew for a fact that she had spent the entire day playing tea party yesterday.

Unfortunately, the way he knew that was a fact was that he was forced to dress up and play with her too. He remembered her smiling impishly as she carefully applied lipstick onto his lips, smearing the majority of the red, sticky substance onto the lower half of his jaw in the process. She then applied some red powder to his cheeks, finishing with a messy swipe of blue on his eyelids. The lipstick smelled like cherries.

It did not, however, taste like cherries. It tasted like crayons.

He scowled as he recalled how hard it was for him to scrub the makeup off his face.

To make things even worse, the class bully, Andy Thomas, had to point out to the entire class that day at recess that he still had a bit of eye shadow on.

A breeze drifted in from the open window nearby, disrupting his thought process for a moment. He could hear the kindergarteners playing by the play structure nearby. Oh, how he wished that he could be out there playing with them. He sighed.

Instead, he had to endure this test.

A test that he had completely forgotten about until Mr. Hall had announced it in class.

"Bobby Brooks. Turn around before I give you an F on your test," Mr. Hall threatened.

With a final glower at Emily, he harrumphed and turned around. She smiled sweetly at him in return.

Bobby rubbed his temples as he turned his attention back to his test. According to his watch (his latest, most prized possession), he had about twenty minutes left.

Suddenly, he recalled Mr. Hall explaining the process of long division clearly in his mind. Glancing at the numbers, he began to smile as it all began to make sense. Ducking his head down, he quickly scribbled the answer onto his paper, moving swiftly to the next problem.

Tap. Tap. Tap.

He chewed on the end of his pencil as he read the next math problem. Ah, multiplication. He liked multiplication.

Tap. Tap. Tap.

He glanced at his watch once more, checking the time. He had about seven minutes left. He nodded to himself; only three more questions to go.

Tap. Tap. Tap.

"Stop making that noise!" Emily exclaimed, exasperated.

"Sorry," Bobby mumbled as he concentrated on the math problem before him.

Tap. Tap. Tap.

"I said, stop it!"

"That wasn't me!"

"Yes, it was!"

"Bobby! Emily! Stop disrupting the rest of the class before I put you both down for detention!" Mr. Hall warned, brandishing his red pen. The two snapped back to their respective places, keen on avoiding detention with Mr. Hall.

Tap. Tap. Tap.

"Bobby!"

"That really wasn't me!" Bobby insisted, throwing his hands up in the air to show his innocence.

Tap. Tap. Tap.

With his hands still in the air, Bobby turned his head towards the source of the tapping.

"Oh, no," he whispered to himself. He slowly turned his gaze to the window. There, right by the windowsill, stood a lone pigeon. It cocked its head to the side, eyeing Bobby with an evil glint in its eye.

You have no power here, Bobby thought smugly to himself. There was no possible way that the pigeon could get into the classroom. Not unless it was planning on pecking its way through the window.

And that simply wasn't possible. Was it?

Bobby quickly finished the last question on his test, beaming with pride. He began to get up to hand his test over.

"Who left that window open? It's too cold!" said Mr. Hall. "Bobby, would you mind shutting that for me?"

Bobby froze in his tracks. The window was open? That must mean…

Tap. Tap. Tap.

He turned around, slowly. The pigeon was perched just outside, lying in wait.

He dashed towards the window, tripping over Andy Thomas's leg in his haste. He couldn't help but smirk as he heard Andy howl in pain.

His smirk faded as the pigeon's head popped through the gap of the open window. He pulled himself up, racing to get to the window.

The pigeon lifted its leg slowly, watching the boy stumble his way across the maze of desks in amusement.

Bobby cursed as he tripped and stubbed his toe on the corner of a chair. He heard a sickening crunch as he threw his arm out in front of him to break his fall. His watch's face had cracked with the force of his body landing on it. He stifled a cry as he got up once more, determined to make it to the window in time.

The pigeon blinked at Bobby, tauntingly holding its leg over the threshold of the window.

Bobby jumped over a pencil case. Only a few steps more… The pigeon stepped inside. "Croo," it announced its arrival.

The pigeon was met with the screeches and shrieks of third graders. Papers shuffled as the children ran to the opposite side of the room.

The room was in utter mayhem. Mr. Hall was nowhere to be seen.

Bobby stood, still rooted to his spot. There was nothing between him and the pigeon except his test paper.

"Croo."

Bobby whimpered in fear.

"Please don't hurt me," Bobby whispered pleadingly.

"Croo," the pigeon stepped closer to him, ruffling its feathers.

Bobby cried, throwing his test paper at the pigeon in panic as he scrambled to join his classmates at the other side of the room.

The pigeon stood motionless as it watched the test paper flutter to the ground.

Bobby watched as the pigeon hopped off the windowsill and sailed to the ground, walking over to the test paper.

"Where is Mr. Hall?" one of the children wailed.

The pigeon raised its head and locked eyes with Bobby as it stepped directly onto the test paper. It stayed there for a tension-filled moment before flapping its wings and making its way out of the window.

Bobby let out a sigh of relief. There seemed to be no damage done.

"Well, that was pretty anti-climactic," said Emily as she walked back to her seat. Bobby shrugged as he retrieved his paper from the ground.

He frowned as his fingers landed on something wet. Sure enough, the pigeon had pooped onto his test paper. There was no way Mr. Hall was accepting his test now.

"And your time is up," announced Mr. Hall as he casually walked back into the classroom, blissfully unaware of the mayhem that had just occurred. "Please hand me your test papers."

"But—" Bobby began to protest. "No exceptions, Bobby. Now."

Outside, the pigeon merrily perched itself on a branch, watching as the smaller human was berated by the larger one as he refused to give his paper in. The larger human snatched the paper away and made a sound of disgust as his fingers smeared the faeces all over the smaller human's written answers. The pigeon cooed happily as the larger human angrily discarded the paper into the trash.

Ah yes, its work here was done for the day.

The pigeon flapped its wings and flew away, leaving the melancholy boy be.

For now.

Pigeons are social creatures that live in groups of up to 30.

High School Drama

"So, who are you going to ask out to the prom?" asked Emily. Bobby scoffed.

"Are you kidding? Me, going to the prom?" said Bobby disdainfully. "I doubt they'll even let me in."

"Oh, come on, Bobby! Don't be so negative!"

"Fine. I'll be lucky if they let me in," said Bobby, rolling his eyes.

"That's the spirit," Emily nodded, taking a bite out of her apple.

Bobby sighed, feeling miserable. Every time he tried to approach a girl for prom, they either fled in terror, or had some misfortune befall them.

And every time misfortune struck, he could have sworn that a pigeon was lurking about.

"I'm telling you, Em. Those pigeons are the ones responsible for everything that has ever gone wrong in my life," he said melancholically.

"You're being so dramatic," said Emily. "You can't just blame everything on pigeons. Don't you know how ridiculous you sound?"

Bobby stared at her in disbelief. "I've known you since we were little kids! Are you telling me that all this time, you've never seen the cause of all my accidents?"

"Bobby," Emily looked at him seriously. "I've told you like a hundred times, the only thing that I've ever seen was an accident-prone dolt who had a knack for getting into some serious sticky situations. And I mean that literally. Yes, there are several events where you are covered in pigeon poop, but that's not the worst thing that could happen to a person."

"You're kidding," Bobby shook his head. "I don't understand why no one ever believes me about this. I don't even know what I did to deserve this," he said, concentrating on the task at hand.

"Maybe if you stopped focusing on your art project and spent more time on figuring out who you could ask out to prom, you wouldn't be so miserable," Emily pointed out.

"Why don't *you* just come with me to the prom?" he asked suddenly. "It would be fun!"

Emily was just about to answer when she felt something touch her shoulder. She brushed her shoulder absent-mindedly as she focused on finding a way to answer Bobby. "Er, you missed the leaf on your shoulder," said Bobby, brushing the fallen leaf off for her.

"Bobby, I'd love to go with you," she sighed. "But Andy already asked me to go, and I told him I would." She shrugged her shoulders at him. Bobby's jaw dropped.

"Andy? Andy Thomas? You can't tell me that you're going to prom with my arch-nemesis! Why can't you just ditch Andy and come with me to prom?" Bobby whined.

"Because Andy asked me out, already. And he already bought a tie to match my outfit," she replied nonchalantly, examining her fingernails as she took another bite of her apple.

"Yeah, but *Andy Thomas*? Really?"

"Whatever rivalry you two have going on with each other is none of my business," said Emily, finishing the last of her apple. Bobby grumbled, smearing glue angrily on the piece of fabric he was working on before sprinkling some glitter for an added touch. "What are you working on, anyway?"

"I have to get this outfit done for the Theatre program. I'm making costumes for the school play." Bobby sighed as he threaded a needle.

"But why are *you* working on it? I thought you hated anything that was related to school activities," said Emily.

"I got into some trouble last week when I accidentally set the theatre club's equipment on fire."

There was a moment of silence as Emily stared at Bobby in disbelief.

"That was you?" Emily said finally, her eyebrows raised. "I heard that that fire did some pretty serious damage."

"It did. To my reputation," Bobby scowled. "Now everyone thinks that I'm some sort of pyromaniac. And I have to remake all of the costumes that were destroyed in the fire as punishment."

"Bobby, how did that happen? I just—I don't—*how*?"

Bobby finished threading his needle and began sewing two pieces of cloth together. "You wouldn't believe me, so there's no point in telling you."

"Why would I not believe you?" asked Emily. Bobby looked at her pointedly.

"It's the pigeons," he whispered at her.

Emily stared at him again.

"Really? You're really going to pin this one on the pigeons too?" Emily asked in disbelief.

"Yes."

"Okay, I'll humour you. What happened?"

"Well, it all started with my audition for the school play…"

Bobby grumbled grumpily to himself as he walked towards the theatre club's room. He hated the fact that he was even going to attempt to audition for the school play, but it was the only way he figured he could score a date for the upcoming prom.

Besides, girls love actors, right?

He read over the script, his nose buried in the papers as he quickly tried to memorize his lines before it was his turn to audition.

"Hi, you're Bobby, right?" said a voice behind him. He turned around to see the most beautiful girl he had ever seen: Michelle Jones. She was in almost every class of his since the beginning of freshman year, but she had never even given him the time of day. He had spent many a day sobbing over her on Emily's shoulder.

"Uh, no… I mean, yeah! That's me!" Bobby stammered nervously. She smiled back at him. His heart skipped a beat.

"Great! I thought I recognized you from History. You're auditioning for the school play?" she asked, tucking a lock of hair behind her ear. He glanced at the shuffled papers in his hand and anxiously tightened his grasp on them. Would she think he was cool for auditioning? What if she thought he was lame? What if— No, he had to play this cool. He smiled at her.

"Uh, are you?" he asked evasively, running a hand through his hair in an attempt to look cool. He'd seen a few guys do it before, although he never really understood why they did it. It always ruined his hair when he tried.

Why would anyone want to deliberately ruin their hair when they wanted to impress a girl? He worked so hard in the morning to get the parting in his hair *exactly* in the middle.

"Oh, no. I wouldn't be caught dead auditioning for the school play," Michelle scoffed, tossing her hair over her shoulder. "I'm just here to get a good laugh at the dorks who bothered to show up to this audition."

Bobby's cheeks flared bright red at her words. "Uh, yeah," he chuckled tensely. "Me too. Ha-ha." He tugged at his collar, loosening up the top button.

"Anyway, I was wondering if you could help me out with the history assignment that's due tomorrow…" She batted her eyes at him, smiling sweetly.

"Bobby," a stern-looking woman called out from the other side of the room. "Please proceed to your audition."

Bobby gulped inwardly as he ignored his call for audition, hoping that Michelle had not heard it.

She did, however.

Michelle raised an eyebrow at him. "You're being called."

"Bobby," the stern woman called again.

"Uh, no I'm not," said Bobby quickly. "She must be talking about another Bobby." He smiled uneasily. "I definitely did not sign up for this play. Anyway, about the assignment, I'd be glad to—"

"Bobby Brooks, please proceed to your audition. Now."

Michelle smirked at him. "I'll let you get to your audition."

Bobby huffed in defeat and humiliation, shuffling his feet as he turned away from Michelle.

He blew it. He blew his chance with Michelle.

He turned back to look at her one last time before he went on stage. She was still there, smiling at him.

Did he *really* lose his chance with Michelle?

He never *actually* got to ask her out. Which meant that he still might have a chance.

He walked up to the microphone and prepared himself to recite his lines. He cleared his throat, but just when he was about to open his mouth, a small fluttering sound caught his attention. He snapped his head towards the light structure that was hooked to the ceiling, narrowing his eyes in suspicion. Seeing nothing out of the ordinary, he turned his attention back to the microphone.

Michelle was still there.

He couldn't resist the urge anymore.

"Michelle Jones, will you do the honour of going to the prom with me?" he announced loudly into the microphone. The majority of his sentence was drowned out by the loud screech of microphone feedback, so he repeated his proposal again.

This time, even louder.

Michelle shrunk away in mortification, fleeing for the door.

The faint fluttering sound grew more distinct. He looked up once more.

Ten pigeons were perched innocently on the light structure. He glanced at the windows of the room. To his dismay, they were all open.

"Well, crap," Bobby announced into the microphone.

And that, unfortunately, was exactly what rained down on him. In his panic to attempt to shield himself from the shower of pigeon excrements, he bumped into some of the sound equipment that was set up.

"My eye! It got in my eye!" Bobby cried out in pain and disgust. He blindly tripped over a wire, sending sparks everywhere which led to the curtain catching on fire.

Bobby, finally getting the excrement out of his eye, watched in horror as the entire stage went up in flames, sending the rest of the students into a rampage as they fled for safety.

Emily laughed, interrupting Bobby's story. "No way," she guffawed, wiping a tear from her eye.

"I'm not kidding," said Bobby miserably. "Every time I asked someone out to the prom, I got pooped on by pigeons—*stop laughing!*"

"I can't help it! Alright, Bobby, I'll go to the prom with you," she said, her laughter dying down with his venomous glare directed at her.

Another leaf landed on her shoulder as she finished uttering her sentence. She lifted a hand to brush it off again, when her hand hit something unexpected. A familiar fluttering sound was heard off in the distance.

"Oh my god!" Bobby cried in disgust. "Why would you touch that?"

"Touch what?" she cried back, trying to crane her neck to see exactly what she touched.

"Bird poop! You just touched bird poop!" he howled. "It's on your shoulder!"

"Bobby! Shut up! People can hear you!" Emily hissed at him. "You're embarrassing me!"

Bobby, however, was not listening to her. He took off running, going as fast as his legs could carry him. "Nowhere is safe! The pigeons are everywhere!" he hollered as he plowed through a group of teenagers standing in the courtyard.

Unfortunately for Bobby, he did not see another pigeon landing directly in his path. His momentum carried him forward, and he could not stop himself in time before he tripped over the pigeon, falling face first in a pile of wet paint.

Or what he thought was wet paint.

He picked himself off of the ground, wiping his eyes clean. "Croo."

"You've got to be kidding me," he whispered to himself as he craned his neck to the source of the noise.

Up there, perched a few feet on a ledge above his head, was a whole flock of pigeons.

"Well," said Bobby for the second time that day. "Crap." And again, for the second time that week, that was exactly what he was covered in.

Pigeons can fly at remarkable speeds, averaging at 77 miles per hour, with the fastest recorded speed clocking at 92 miles per hour.

A Really, Really Bad Day

Bobby sighed as he walked into his dingy apartment, wincing as the doorframe shuddered under the force of his slamming the door. He set his hat down onto a wobbly coffee table and made his way to the kitchen, his stomach rumbling with hunger. He hadn't eaten all day, despite the fact that he worked as a chef in a restaurant. Or at least, he *used* to work as a chef in a restaurant.

Bobby had shown up to work late that day. He struggled to pull his head through his apron and fumbled with the strings for a few moments before finally securing them into a knot. Straightening his chef's hat as he rushed into the kitchen, he steered himself over to his station, ducking out of the way of his other bustling co-workers.

"Order up!" a busboy yelled through the midst, thrusting a list of pizzas that he was to make for a table into his hand. He raised an eyebrow as he scanned through the list.

"Thirteen pies for table seven?" Bobby said, his eyebrows furrowing in bewilderment. "How many people are at this table, exactly?"

The busboy snickered, pointing his thumb behind him at two individuals seated at a table in the corner.

Bobby's eyes widened as he took in the size of the two customers; the man was so large that his five chins wobbled while he reprimanded his equally as large son for picking his nose in public. The boy shook his head furiously and banged his fist on the table in protest as the man physically tried to pry his hand away from his nose.

The boy, however, managed to push his finger further up his nose. The man sighed and sat back in his seat in defeat, letting the boy pick his nose in peace. The boy seemed to have dug his finger so far deep into his nostril that he had trouble getting his finger out of his nose, and began to wail loudly in response.

Shaking his head, Bobby went back to rolling out the pizza dough, stretching it out and tossing it into the air. Catching the pie artfully, he slapped it onto the table and began to pour marinara sauce over the dough.

His heart fluttered as he caught Emily's eye, who had started working as the new waitress just the week before.

He had never realized how beautiful she actually was… After spending all that time together, it was bound to happen, he mused. Now, what would be the best way that he could get her attention?

He tried to wink at her while splashing some more sauce onto the pizza. Unfortunately, he managed to miss the pizza entirely, and the sauce ended up all over his chef's uniform. He let out a rather girly shriek as the hot sauce stained through his clothes and burned his skin. He flung the ladle he was using into the air and ripped his shirt off, sighing in relief as the heat from the sauce disappeared from his body.

He was suddenly aware that he had no shirt on, and sped off to find another shirt to wear.

Alas, he could not find another appropriate shirt to wear, and quickly had to fashion a shirt from several dirty washcloths from the dishwasher's station before the manager had noticed.

Grinning sheepishly as he re-entered the kitchen, he nodded at his co-workers curtly and got back to his station. As he finished putting the last of the mozzarella cheese onto the thirteenth pizza pie, Emily waltzed into the kitchen once more.

"Hi, Emily," he stammered as she flashed him a dazzling smile. He was so entranced by her beauty that he did not realize how far he had pushed the pizza pies into the firewood oven.

The silly grin was still stretched across his face as smoke suddenly began billowing out of the oven, filling the entire kitchen with the thick smoke at an alarming rate.

"Fire!" he yelled. He tried to put the fire out by pulling his towel-shirt over his head and throwing it into the oven as well, hoping to smother the fire.

Sadly, the towels caught fire as well, triggering the smoke alarm and water sprinklers.

"Everybody, out!" the manager barked as he stormed through the kitchen. "Follow protocol and have the entire restaurant evacuated before someone sues us for every penny we're worth!"

Bobby raced to the front of the restaurant and guided the customers out, accidentally trampling on quite a few feet in the process.

Finally, the restaurant had been fully evacuated and the fire department had arrived to fish out the blackened remains of the pizza. Bobby sighed in relief.

His relief was short-lived as he saw the manager approach him. He gulped.

"How did this happen, Bobby?" the manager demanded, angrily.

"Why are you asking me? It could have been anyone!" he argued, slightly offended that he would be the first to be questioned. The manager scoffed.

"You are the most accident-prone employee that I had ever had the misfortune to hire. Tell me that it wasn't you," he dared Bobby. Bobby opened his mouth to retaliate, but then closed it as he realized that he really was at fault.

"I should fire you," the manager seethed at Bobby. "I should fire you and make sure that you will never find work in this town again. But you're lucky that I actually need you as a chef." The manager sighed. Bobby held his breath, anticipating another lecture.

The manager shook his head and put a hand on Bobby's shoulder. "These things happen. Just don't let it happen again." Bobby watched in bewilderment as the manager walked away.

He was safe! He wasn't fired!

His attention was turned to the fireman who was announcing that it was safe to return to the restaurant, as the fire had been contained. The customers filed in, eager to receive their free meals that were promised by the manager to accommodate for the inconvenience.

"Alright, everyone! Back to work," the manager barked as he herded the employees back into the restaurant.

Bobby scowled as he noticed the two large customers that were behind the order of the pizzas that were responsible for the fire in the first place. They were happily trudging back into the restaurant, which meant that he had to remake their orders once more.

Bobby was so busy glaring daggers at the two that he did not see the pigeon that was hopping about and picking up scraps from the side of the road. His foot landed right in front of the pigeon, emitting an alarmed "croo."

Startled, Bobby veered away from the pigeon and tripped over the curb, landing face first into a muddy puddle.

Unfortunately, the large man happened to be in the way. He shrieked as mucky drops of water rained down onto him. "My shirt! It's ruined!" he cried, outraged.

"I'm so sorry, sir!" Bobby stammered out his apologies, mopping up the mud off of him with his apron. He was met with another shriek, this time with a more hysterical note.

"I am a *woman*! Oh, I've never been so insulted in my *life*! I'll sue!" she cried.

Bobby was just about ready to collapse from sheer embarrassment. Could this day get any worse?

"Ma'am, I sincerely apologize for my incompetent, nincompoop employee's behaviour," the manager cried as he rushed over, overhearing Bobby's exchange with the customer. He pushed the mortified Bobby away from the woman before he had any bodily harm inflicted onto him.

Bobby winced. He was sure to get into more trouble for this mishap.

"I'm sure this was all a big misunderstanding," the manager said smoothly, patting the woman's arm. "Here, let me bring you the house's best cocktail, and some orange juice for your son."

Seeming to be satisfied with the manager's grovelling, the woman harrumphed and allowed herself to be led back into the restaurant.

"Go get the drinks," the manager hissed at Bobby.

Bobby nodded and rushed into the kitchen, emerging with a tray laden with assorted colourful drinks.

He knew that his job was on the line, now.

Bobby's hand trembled as he set the tray down, feeling the burning glare he was receiving from the woman.

Unfortunately, he managed to spill the drinks all over her sleeve, which provoked yet another outraged shriek from the woman. She waved her arms around as she showered him with such creative profanities that he had almost forgotten to take offense.

Just as she was about to storm out of the restaurant, a large flambé made its way out of the kitchen, heading straight towards them.

Bobby saw everything happen as if it were in slow motion; the woman's fancy sleeve flew through the air and plunged into the dessert that was currently aflame. Her eyes widened in shock as the flames travelled up her arm. She proceeded to run around in a circle, waving her arm about as she tried to put the fire out, accidentally lighting nearby tablecloths in the process.

"Stop, drop and roll!" the woman's son yelled, throwing himself onto her and knocking her to the ground. She took his advice to heart and began rolling around on the floor, still shrieking. Her son's yells joined her shrieks as she managed to roll on top of him several times, blocking his airflow, effectively knocking him out.

Bobby quickly dialled 911 while the manager evacuated the restaurant once more.

The entire restaurant was quite a scene by the time the day came to an end. The ambulance carted the son away and the fire department arrived to spray the woman down with an extinguisher, covering her in a thick blanket of white foam.

Panting, she heaved herself up off of the ground, wiping the thick foam out of her eyes. Unfortunately, her rather heavy foot landed onto the fireman's foot, and he cried out in pain and hurled the fire extinguisher into the air. Bobby's jaw dropped open in horror as he saw the fire extinguisher sail through the air and hit his manger squarely on the face.

Silence echoed throughout the entire vicinity.

"That is *it*!" the manager yelled, furious. "Bobby, come over here." He stomped his foot onto the floor and pointed in front of him.

Bobby gulped and made his way slowly to his manager. "Sir, should I have the paramedics take a look at your head?" he asked quietly, looking at the bump on his head that was rapidly growing to the size of a grapefruit.

The manager shook his head, his face turning crimson as his anger grew. Suddenly, Bobby was overtaken with the desire to laugh as a thought occurred to him: his manger was beginning to resemble an overripe, veiny tomato.

Not being able to help himself, he let out a guffaw, which stopped as quickly as it started as he realized that that was probably the last thing he should have done.

The day ended with his apron being ripped off of him by his manager and stomped over. The woman joined in, digging her feet into the apron with such enthusiasm that it was quickly reduced to tattered pieces of cloth.

Bobby arrived home feeling so depressed and weighed down with the cruel label of being a failure that he hadn't even bothered to take off his clothes before stepping into the shower. He stared unseeingly in front of him as the water rained down onto his head, soaking his entire attire.

He suddenly realized in horror that he had forgotten to take off his expensive watch, which was sadly unwater-proofed. He raised his wrist to check if his watch was still working.

To his dismay, the platinum-plated second hand was completely stationary. He let out a groan, banging his head on the wall behind him in frustration. After he was done, he reached for the bar of soap that was sitting in the soap dish. His grip was so hard that the bar slipped right out of his hands and landed squarely on his left toe, to which he yelled out in pain and clutched his toe in agony. He quickly realized his mistake of trying to balance on one foot in the shower, and set his foot back down before he had lost his balance.

Unfortunately, he set his foot onto the bar of soap, which sent him sliding out of the shower and across the bathroom. He put his arm out to steady himself against the wall, but missed and ended up plunging his entire arm into the toilet, which he coincidentally forgot to flush after using.

He stared at his filth-covered hand in disbelief. A drop of water splattered onto the floor as he lifted his hand towards his face, soiling the tiled floor.

This was the last straw.

Bobby shook his head and decided that he would just end things then and there.

Life just wasn't worth living anymore.

He got up, not bothering to clean the faeces staining his skin, and pulled out a hair dryer. He slowly plugged it into the socket and stepped into the shower. Taking a deep breath, he reached out to turn the water on.

Just as his hand touched the tap, a small "pop" sounded, and he was thrown into darkness. Realizing what had just happened, he let out an agonized scream.

The power had just gone out, foiling his plan to end his misery.

He stepped out of the shower, grumbling furiously to himself as he unplugged the hairdryer (although he had also felt slightly relieved that his plan hadn't worked after all).

A thought suddenly occurred to him. What if this was a sign? What if he had been saved for a reason?

Bobby smiled.

"Perhaps being a failure isn't quite so bad. After all, everything happens for a reason," he said to himself.

Cheering up, he hummed a tune as he made his way to the door.

Unfortunately, Bobby's misfortune struck again. He stepped onto the wretched bar of soap once more, which sent him slipping and sliding all the way across the bathroom and right out the window. Bobby screamed as he sailed down ten stories, convinced that he was facing certain doom. His scream halted when he landed onto a dumpster stuffed to the brim with mattresses, which broke his fall.

He sat up in disbelief, marvelling at his survival.

"I'm alive?" he asked no one in particular, feeling himself all over for any broken limbs. Finding none, he jumped up for joy and clapped his hands.

"This proves it!" he exclaimed happily. "I have been saved for a reason! I am destined for great things." He grinned.

Bobby resolved to do more important things with his life. His near-death experience had certainly opened his eyes.

Perhaps he should read more.

He stopped at a newspaper stand and flipped through a magazine. That would be a good start.

"Interesting," he thought aloud to himself. "A pigeon never forgets a face…" he read. "I've heard that before, somewhere…" he mused.

Shrugging, he put the magazine back onto the racks and fished out a couple of dollars for a cup of coffee.

He looked up after taking a large sip to see a pigeon standing in front of him, its beady eyes boring into him.

Recalling that he had almost stepped on a pigeon earlier that day, he gulped. Suddenly, another pigeon settled next to it, and then another.

Soon, an entire flock of pigeons were blocking his path on the sidewalk. Bobby took a step forward, watching the pigeons wearily as they all seemed to take a unified step towards him. Gulping nervously again, he took another step towards them before dashing in the opposite direction.

A woman across the street covered her son's eyes as she watched in horror at the sight before her: a man was being swallowed by a large, mottled white-and-grey cloud of flapping, croo-ing beings, his screams and cries for help drowned out by the sound of the pigeons as they attacked the poor man.

Pigeons mate for a lifetime.

A female pigeon lays two eggs that hatch after eighteen days.

The offspring is dependent on both parents for the first two months of their lives.

A Conspiracy

Emily sighed, closing her eyes for a moment as she felt the wind ripple through her hair. She felt exhausted; it had been a long time since she had had a proper night's sleep.

"KEEP YOUR EYES ON THE ROAD! ON THE ROAD!"

Emily snapped out of her daze and turned her attention back to the task at hand, tightening her grip on the wheel. "Chill, Bobby," she huffed, annoyed. "I know what I'm doing."

"Apparently not," Bobby said, crossing his arms stubbornly in the passenger's seat. "We're never going to escape the farmers if you keep sticking your head out of the window like that! We're probably just going to end up in a ditch somewhere on the side of the road at this rate. What are you thinking, closing your eyes in the middle of driving the car?"

Emily glared at Bobby as she pressed her heel to the gas pedal. Bobby winced as the engine whined beneath the strain that they were putting it under.

"Well, this isn't my fault! And besides, can you roll your window down? It smells in here!" she cringed, wrinkling her nose.

"But it's cold! I don't want to roll down my window," Bobby whined. He was silenced by her silent death glare.

"Well, *someone* wanted to stop by the burrito stand on the way to the pigeon farm, and it smells awful—" Emily began, flipping her short hair behind her shoulders.

"Hey! I was hungry, and that burrito stand was the only source of food for miles," Bobby sniffed. "It was either the burrito stand, or nothing!"

"Bobby, when there are rat droppings *on the chef's ladle*, the answer is nothing."

"Nonsense. Those were probably just dried beans or something. There is no way someone would have a burrito stand infested with rats," insisted Bobby, taking another bite of his burrito. Emily watched as the beans dripped from his chin and dribbled onto her leather seats. She groaned inwardly. She just had the car cleaned…

"Well," Emily huffed. "I'm not stopping anywhere else, so don't ask me for any bathroom breaks or any other pit stops."

"But what if I really have to go to the bathroom?"

"Well, that would be too bad, but I'm definitely not stopping. You're a grown man. You can hold it," Emily replied.

"I don't see why we can't even stop for the bathroom," said Bobby indignantly.

"Gee, I don't know, Bobby. Maybe it would be easier if we weren't being chased by a bunch of pigeon farmers?" Emily said sarcastically.

Sure enough, there was a horde of farmers rampaging the roads behind them, a cloud of dust billowing out behind the pickup trucks that were racing after the couple.

"Er- right," he replied sheepishly. "Just out of curiosity, what is the worst that could happen if they caught us?" Bobby asked, wincing as their tires flew over a pothole in the road. The road seemed to stretch out forever in front of them, with nothing but deserted marshlands on either side. "It's not like they're going to prod us with pitchforks, or throw us into a pit of livestock for punishment," said Bobby. He braced himself as they hit another pothole. "Slow down, Emily! You're going to get us both killed!"

"No, Bobby! We could get arrested for what we did," said Emily.

"Arrested? I don't think we'd get arrested. We didn't do anything *that* bad —" he was silenced with another glare from Emily.

"Bobby," she said slowly. "We raided a government-run pigeon farm and stole a whole truckload of pigeons!"

"Well, I *told* you, I'm certain that pigeons are the creation of the government! They can't be natural creatures. I can't live the rest of my life thinking that I have spies from the government surrounding me, watching my every move…" Bobby trailed off, looking paranoid.

"Tell me again, *why* do you think that pigeons are the creation of the government?" asked Emily, her eyes glancing at the rear-view mirror. She could see the angry farmers shaking their fists at them from their own vehicle, shrieking insults at the couple.

"Think about it, Emily," said Bobby. "Think of all the pigeons out there. They're all the same. Have you ever seen a pigeon that was different in size, or colour? Have you ever seen a baby pigeon? Or have you ever seen pigeons doing anything other than walking around, bobbing their evil little heads as they walk around, or poop on people?" Bobby whispered at Emily, drawing his face closer and closer with each word. Emily rolled her eyes again. With his ruffled black hair and his ripped shirt, stained with dirt and bird excrements, he looked like he a madman. She looked down at herself for a moment, examining the dirt stains that were on her own clothes. She supposed she looked just as bad as he did, if not worse. One of those pesky pigeons had gotten loose while they were loading the cages up into her trunk and pooped onto her head as it flew away.

"I still think that they're just birds, and you're just a little insane," she said, anxiously looking back at the farmers. They seemed to be almost losing their trail.

"Then how do you think the FBI or the CIA get all of their information? It's genius, really. I'm telling you, it's from the pigeons. They're everywhere!"

"That's just absurd, Bobby," she told him exasperatedly. "The FBI and the CIA probably use databases and criminal records! Not *pigeons*, of all things!"

"If it's so absurd, then why did you come help me raid the pigeon farm?" Bobby smirked.

"I came because I think that somehow, the pigeons have formed some kind of vendetta against you and are plotting your demise. How else would you explain everything that's been going on? It's the only conclusion that makes any sense," she stated matter-of-factly.

"And how does that theory sound any less absurd than mine?" Bobby pointed out. Emily opened her mouth to retaliate but then closed it, finding nothing for her defence.

"Fine," she huffed, defeated. "But I didn't think we'd get caught!"

"Well, how was I supposed to know that today was the annual Pigeon Farmer's Banquet?" Bobby shifted in his seat uncomfortably. Emily sighed.

"I told you to research everything before we went to raid the farm!"

"How was I supposed to know that there was even such a thing as the annual Pigeon Farmer's Banquet? And besides, if pigeons *are* part of a government conspiracy, it would never show up on the Internet!"

Emily sighed exasperatedly, shaking her head in incredulity.

They fell silent for a moment; the only audible sound was the ruffling of the distressed pigeons in their cages that were chained in place in the back of the pickup truck. Bobby turned his head to peer back at the poor birds.

"Did you line the back of my pickup truck with newspaper?" Emily asked, bringing Bobby back from his train of thought.

"Yeah, I put the newspaper in the back. It was yesterday's edition, though," said Bobby.

"Why would I care what edition it was? I just need it to protect my trunk from bird poop."

"Oh. I just thought you wanted to read it," said Bobby absentmindedly. "That makes more sense, though."

"Wait, so you just put the newspaper in the back?" asked Emily.

"Yeah."

"You didn't cover my trunk in it?"

"Er- I think I might have forgotten to do that," he said quietly, wincing at the certain lecture he was going to be faced with.

"You forgot?" repeated Emily, her anger rising. "You forgot to do the *one* thing that told you to do? Do you realize what is going to happen now?"

"The back of your pickup truck is going to be covered in bird droppings by the time we get out of here," Bobby promptly replied. Emily groaned.

"This day just keeps on getting better and better," she sighed. She glanced back at the farmers, who were still on their trail. Her eyes widened as she realized how close they were getting. She pressed her foot onto the gas pedal once more.

"Uh, not to make things any worse, but I think we're also running out of gas," said Bobby as he nervously glanced at the gas meter, the blinking E catching his eye.

"Well, we have no other choice than to keep going," Emily shook her head. "I can't get arrested for stealing *pigeons* of all things. I'll be the laughing stock of the town! I can't be known as the girl who went to jail for stealing birds."

"They aren't birds. They are spy drones from the government!" argued Bobby.

"Bobby, they are *not* spy drones from the government," she argued back. "They are just evil little birds who—"

"Shhhh!" Bobby hissed at her. "They can hear you!"

"I am going to throw you out of this car if I hear one more mention of spy droids—"

"Drones," Bobby corrected.

"Drones! Whatever, Bobby! One more word, and I'm throwing you out," Emily threatened.

The couple enjoyed a few moments of silence before it was interrupted by a loud rumble. Emily and Bobby both turned towards the source of the noise: Bobby's stomach.

"Uh, you weren't serious when you said we weren't stopping for any bathroom breaks, were you?" asked Bobby hesitantly.

"I was one hundred percent serious. Why?" Emily asked slowly.

"Because I *really* need to use the bathroom," Bobby said, stretching his lips into a queasy smile.

"Seriously?" "Seriously."

"I already told you, Bobby, we can't pull over!" Emily cried. "Who knows what those farmers would do to us! They've been following us for the past hour."

"I can't believe they've been following us for this long. You'd think they would have called the police by now," Bobby mused.

"Bobby," she said suddenly. "Why *haven't* they called the cops? I mean, if I were in their place, that would have been my first move."

Bobby and Emily looked at each other for a moment in realization.

"I was right," Bobby whispered. "I can't believe it. I was right!"

"I can't believe I'm saying this, but I think I'm starting to believe you," Emily peered warily at the back of her pickup truck. A pigeon was staring back at her, its black eyes blinking at her ominously. "Croo," it cooed at her, suddenly pecking at the cage's wires.

Bobby burped loudly, snapping her out of her daze. She looked over at Bobby to see him holding his stomach in pain. "I think I'm going to be sick."

"Oh, no," Emily wailed. "Not in the car! I just had it cleaned yesterday!"

"I need a bag, then!" he cried, another rumble ripping its way out of his belly.

"I don't have a bag! You're going to have to wait, unless you have a better idea."

"Well, I think I can think of one solution," said Bobby slowly. He looked at Emily pointedly, waiting for her to follow his thoughts. It took her a moment, and her eyes narrowed at him dangerously.

"Don't you dare."

"But why not?" asked Bobby. "I don't see why I can't do it, it seems like a perfectly good idea."

Emily sighed, dropping her head into both of her hands. This was probably the most horrid day of her life. The pigeons, this conversation, her car…

"THE ROAD! THE ROAD!" Bobby yelled, grabbing onto the wheel from the passenger's seat as the car began swivelling off the side of the road.

"Sorry!" she cried, snapping her head up and grasping the wheel, correcting their course.

"So, can I do it? We don't have a bag, and it's a perfectly good alternative idea!" Bobby said after a few moments of gasping for air.

"No! And I'm not going to sit here and explain to you why it's a bad idea," said Emily, sounding exasperated. "Common sense should suffice as enough reason!"

"But I did it one time before!" Bobby whined. "You seemed to think it was a perfectly good idea then!"

"Bobby, the last time you did that, you were almost arrested for indecent exposure! We do not need one more charge to add to this possible arrest, so I need you to keep your mouth shut," she said through gritted teeth, pinching the bridge of her nose as she tried to calm herself down.

Silence ensued for the next couple of minutes. "Can I at least *try* doing it—" Bobby began.

"No!"

"It's not like I'm going to hurt anyone if I do!"

"It's illegal!" Emily burst out angrily. "It's bad enough we're still being chased by those farmers. If your theory on pigeons is correct, then that means we've just stolen property from the government! And now we are being chased by the people we stole from! *And* we're running out of gas!" she cried, exasperated. "Why did I even agree to this?" she moaned.

"You lost the coin toss!"

"I didn't care about the stupid coin toss! You blackmailed me into going along with you!"

"Did not! I merely mentioned that I would accidentally drop your phone in the toilet if I didn't have my way."

"Bobby. You were actually holding my phone over the toilet. With two fingers. That's blackmail."

"Oh… Well, then I guess I blackmailed you."

"You're horrible," Emily groaned, dropping her head to rest on the steering wheel.

Bobby moaned, his facial expression morphing into one of anguish as he clutched at his belly.

"Emily. My stomach hurts."

"Oh my God, you're like a child!"

"I can't help it!"

"No one asked you to eat that stupid burrito! In fact, I asked you *not* to!"

"I was hungry!" Bobby shot back.

"Bobby, there were rat droppings everywhere in that burrito stand! We even saw a few rats nearby!" Emily swerved the car to the left suddenly, trying to use an evasive technique to lose the farmers.

"What did you do that for? Now I feel even more sick!"

"The farmers are getting closer! Why don't they just give up? They're just pigeons, anyway!"

"They're spy drones from the government!"

"Bobby, they are *not* spy drones from the government," Emily huffed.

"You just agreed with my theory a few minutes ago! Besides, what other absurd ideas have I had today?" Bobby crossed his arms defiantly. Emily chewed her lip, annoyed.

"First of all: The burrito stand," Emily listed. "Second, suggesting that we raid pigeon farms and steal all of the pigeons! Need I say more?"

Bobby stayed silent, shrinking back in his seat in defeat. "I still feel sick, though," he muttered. She sighed, rummaging a hand in the back and pushing a large paper cup at him.

"If you feel like throwing up, do it in there. I already told you, I just had my car cleaned."

"Er, it's not *that* kind of sick," Bobby told her, his stomach rumbling loudly. She wrinkled her nose in disgust as an unpleasant smell wafted towards her that smelled vaguely of a bean burrito.

"Bobby!" she yelled, gagging.

"Sorry! This would all be over if you would just let me—"

"NO!"

Half an hour had passed in silence since their argument, and Emily enjoyed every second of it. She veered gently into another lane, almost forgetting that the farmers were still chasing after them.

Until...

"OH MY GOD. WHAT IS THAT?" Bobby cried out in panic as something thudded against the hood of their car.

"Is that...?"

"They're hurling pigeon crap at us!" Bobby cried again, rolling his window up as another shot of pigeon faeces was sent flying at them. It narrowly missed the window, landing with a large splat onto the side of the door.

"What? How is that even possible?!"

"I don't know! If pigeons are the creation of the government, then anything is possible at this point!"

"What have we gotten ourselves into?" Emily wailed. "Just step on it! STEP ON IT!" Bobby hollered.

Real panic settled into the car now. Emily thought of all the things that she could lose if the farmers would have caught her. Would she lose her scholarship for college? Would she be sent to jail? Had she really just stolen federal government property?

"*Now* can I do it?" Bobby suddenly asked.

"Do what?" Emily asked, sounding confused for a moment. "Oh. OH. NO! I already told you, NO!"

"But *why*, Emily? Why?"

"Because it's gross, and it's illegal. And we're about to get caught by a bunch of pigeon farmers! Now, if you have anything useful to suggest, speak now. Otherwise, we are going to get ripped apart by those wretched farmers and their pigeons. We need to come up with a plan, because we're going to run out of gas soon." She glanced at the blinking E on the dashboard again.

Bobby thought hard for a moment. Suddenly, he reached over and grabbed at her gearshift, pulling the handle backwards onto reverse. Emily shrieked.

"What are you doing?!" she screamed in terror, feeling the car jerking itself into a sudden stop before zooming backwards onto the road.

"I have an idea!" Bobby cried proudly. "Let's fight fire with fire!" he said as he began rolling his window down again.

"No, Bobby! I know what you're going to do! Don't do it! I told you no before, and I'm going to say no again! No!"

"But it's perfect! It'll help us escape!"

"I said, no!"

"But—"

"FINE! JUST DO IT!" Emily finally screamed, aggravated. "JUST BLOODY DO IT ALREADY AND LET ME DRIVE IN PEACE!"

"R-really?"

"Bobby! Before I change my mind!" she snarled at him. She was running out of gas quickly. "Make sure to aim well."

"Okay!" Bobby cried happily. She rolled his windows down, looking away in horror as he began loosening his belt. "I can't believe you're going to do this," she told him disbelievingly.

She saw the farmers draw closer and closer as her car continued to zoom backwards. Suddenly, she felt a click in gearshift, and she looked down in horror to see that Bobby had kneed it again in his excitement to do what he had been bugging her to do for almost the entirety of their getaway. Their car began to go forwards again, and she felt her neck hit the back of her seat as their vehicle shot in the opposite direction.

"NO NO NO! BOBBY! DON'T DO IT WHILE THE CAR IS GOING FORWARDS! DON'T DO IT WHILE I'M—"

"What's happening?" Bobby wailed, feeling lost at all the chaos that was ensuing around them.

"ROLL UP THE WINDOWS! ROLL UP THE WINDOWS, FOR CRYING OUT LOUD! IT'S GOING TO FLY INTO OUR CAR! IT'S GOIING TO FLY INTO OUR CAR!"

But it was too late.

Bobby let out a satisfied "aah," his face contorted into a very odd expression of relief and satisfaction.

But nothing, *nothing*, could ever match the expressions of the pedestrians and people in traffic alongside with them as they saw Bobby's pale butt sticking out of the window with poop stains on the side of the car from when the wind had blown his excretions back onto the car, rather than onto the farmers.

Except, perhaps, the mortified poop-covered woman in the driver's seat with her window half open.

"MY HAIR! MY BEAUTIFUL HAIR! MY CAR! WHAT HAVE YOU DONE TO MY—"

"Here it comes again!" exclaimed Bobby enthusiastically.

Amidst their panicked screams, neither of them noticed as the cages in the back up of the pickup truck unlatched. The pigeons ruffled their feathers, eyeing their chance of freedom.

"I'm not even going to bother," muttered a policeman as he munched on a donut, eyeing the car zooming on the road with a pale butt sticking out of the side. Behind it, a horde of angry, confused-looking farmers sticking their heads out of a parade of pickup trucks furiously racing behind.

"Not even going to bother…" he muttered, taking another bite out of his chocolate frosted donut. He jerked suddenly, startled at the sound of a woman shrieking. He whipped his head around towards the direction of the voice, only to find a giant cloud of pigeons emerging from the horizon and into the sky, looming ominously like a dark, mottled thundercloud.

"Oh, no. Nuh-uh. Nope," the policeman said, hiking his pants up to his waist and reaching for his car keys. "They don't pay me enough for this!"

He dropped his donut and ran.

A booming roar echoed throughout the vicinity as the pigeon-thundercloud spread across the sky.

"Croo."

Pigeons have incredible hearing abilities. They are able to detect sounds at extremely low frequencies. They can hear distant storms, earthquakes, and volcanic eruptions.

Pigeon Apocalypse

"Honey, I'm heading out again!" Bobby called as he walked towards the door, briefcase in hand.

"Again?" sighed Emily. "You've been working late for the last few weeks. Why don't you stay home for tonight?"

"I already told you, I can't," said Bobby, shaking his head. "I have to get this project finished. I *have* to." Bobby leaned over to give Emily a quick kiss on her cheek before leaving.

She huffed moodily as she began to clear up the dinner table, wrapping up her husband's untouched meal in aluminium foil before putting it into the fridge.

Bobby had been acting strange for the last couple of months—stranger than usual—and it had only begun to grow stranger and stranger as time passed on.

He was an odd man. Then again, he had always been an odd man. He even had a strange way of walking. He would duck his head ever so often as he turned his head this way and that up at the sky, scanning the area with narrowed eyes, as if expecting something to come shooting out from the clouds and barrelling into him.

For good reason. Pigeons had been attacking and harassing Bobby Brooks from the time he was a little boy.

She had originally written his behaviour off as a form of anxiety, and it was easily overshadowed by his overly charming antics.

However, in all of their five years of marriage, he had never been acting *this* strange. He had never been this obsessed with work.

In fact, he hated work.

A familiar padding sound was heard across the room as her dog, Splat, made his way to his water bowl.

Bobby hated the name. He desperately tried to change it, but it was the only name their four-legged friend seemed to respond to.

Whatever could Bobby be doing at work this late? He was working as a mechanic, for crying out loud. Mechanics don't work late as often as he had recently been, do they?

Emily sighed, shaking her head at her paranoia.

She had known Bobby since they were both eight years old. After spending their whole lives together as friends, they had finally fallen in love with each other. He had never given her reason to doubt his loyalty to her.

He was still an odd man, though.

She patted Splat as she made her way towards the couch.

Perhaps curling up on a comfy couch with her favourite book would ease her mind.

She flipped her book open to where she had left off last. Ah, yes, the part where the main character was about to realize the truth…

Splat padded happily towards his master with his tongue lolling out, resting his head onto her lap and waiting for her to scratch his ears. She absentmindedly ran a hand across his head and patted him nonchalantly, completely absorbed into her book.

An hour had passed since she had begun reading. By then, Splat moved away from her with his nose held high in resentment at her less-than-enthusiastic patting. He trotted his way back into the kitchen.

"Aww, Splat! Come back," Emily called after her dog. She leaned over to see where he had gone when a light caught her eye.

The lights were on in the garage.

She frowned. She was certain that she had locked the garage door. There was no one else at home.

She peered out of the window again, staring out at the lights that were coming from the garage's window. Perhaps she had forgotten to turn off the lights when she was in there earlier?

Her train of thought halted as she heard a rattle coming from the garage. She narrowed her eyes, walking over to the closet in the hallway and reaching out for something that she could use as a weapon. Her hands closed around the handle of a baseball bat, and she gripped it tightly as she slowly made her way down to the garage door.

"Splat?" she called out in a hushed whisper. She found the dog huddled up in the corner, whining as she tried to pull at his collar. "Oh, you little coward," she whispered disdainfully at the dog. It stuck its nose up snootily in the air again and turned its back to her, refusing to budge. Emily rolled her eyes, deciding to go and investigate the noise on her own.

As she neared the garage door, the rattling sound grew more distinctive. Someone was definitely inside the garage.

She jutted her jaw out in determination as she took in a few deep breaths. She placed a hand carefully onto the polished doorknob, closing her eyes before taking another step.

Throwing it open, she let out a strangled cry as she brought the bat high up above her head, ready to strike at the unsuspecting intruder. She missed, and the bat landed squarely onto a large mechanical device that was sitting in the corner of the room. Spinning around wildly, she raised the bat again.

"Emily! Emily! No! It's me!" a frantic voice cried out. "Stop trying to hit me!"

Emily opened her eyes, stopping her blind swing just before it struck him on the head. "Bobby? What are you doing in here?!"

"I'm working! That's what I told you before I left!" he cried, sounding bewildered. "Why do you want to hit me with a bat? Did you find the spaghetti stain on the other side of the couch cushion? I swear, I was going to tell you about it, but the sauce crusted over, and then the mould began to settle in, and the smell—"

"What? What stain? No! I thought you were an intruder, and I thought you were going to the office to work!" said Emily, sounding equally as confused. She turned her attention to the grotesquely dismantled mechanical device.

"Well, you obviously misunderstood!" yelled Bobby, his anger and confusion growing. Emily cleared her throat sheepishly as she realized that her mistake was one that of pure stupidity.

She turned her head back towards him as she calmed down and examined the damage. The mechanical device that Bobby had been working on had been smashed horribly. She was immediately flooded with guilt.

"Months' worth of work… down the drain," Bobby said mournfully as he knelt down onto the ground to pick up a few stray bolts and screws. Emily awkwardly knelt down beside him, uncertain of what to say.

"What were you trying to make?" she asked finally.

Bobby sighed sadly. "You wouldn't understand."

"No, tell me. It's the least I could do after I, um, broke your device," Emily said embarrassedly. Bobby looked at her, debating whether to be annoyed at her for destroying his work, or to marvel at her courage for facing a potential intruder with a weapon, ready to drive them out of their home with a baseball bat. He let out another sigh, putting a hand fondly on her shoulder.

"It's my own invention. It's a Pigeon Homing Device. Patent pending."

Emily stared at Bobby, flabbergasted. "A Pigeon Homing Device," she repeated. Bobby nodded solemnly. "Bobby, what on *earth* is a Pigeon Homing Device?"

Bobby gazed up at the ceiling dreamily. "It's my greatest invention yet. It is a device that will attract every pigeon on the planet to this location."

Emily stared at him. "Why would you make something like that? You hate pigeons."

"Exactly! It's brilliant! Once I attract every pigeon on the planet to this location, I can destroy them all, effectively wiping out pigeons from the face of the planet!" Bobby said excitedly.

"Why on earth would you want to do that? I know they do have a tendency to poop on you." Here, Emily stifled a small gulp of laughter, remembering all the times Bobby would have to scrub out dried pigeon poop from his clothes. "But that's no reason to wipe them all out."

"To say that they've been pooping on me is an understatement," said Bobby shortly. "At this point, it literally rains pigeon crap on me. It's ridiculous!" Bobby cried. "Pigeons have been ruining my life ever since I could remember. And I don't even know *why*," Bobby cried, burying his face in his hands.

"Oh, don't be so dramatic," Emily rolled her eyes. "I'm sure that pigeons didn't ruin your life."

"But they did! They made me fail the fourth grade, they ruined prom for me, I got named as a pyromaniac for burning down the theatre set at high school, I got fired from my first job, and they pelted me with pigeon faeces on my way to a very important meeting. For crying out loud, that day was officially named as the Shit Storm at our town!" cried Bobby. "They made weather reports about it! And I am tired of having to wash the slimy goo off of my clothes every single day, and I gave up on washing my car a long time ago. Every time I park my car and leave, I come back to it covered in pigeon poop. I'm just so tired of it all," Bobby fell down to his knees dramatically, bowing his head down in sorrow.

"Oh Bobby, I know that's horrible, but it's not that big of a reason to drive pigeons to extinction…" Emily was thinking about a few comforting words she could say, but he lifted his head abruptly and continued his rant.

"And as if that wasn't enough, I drew the winning card at the lottery last month, which was worth ten million dollars, and a pigeon crapped right on my card. I tried to scrape off the poop, but I ended up scraping off the numbers, and they considered that as tampering with the lottery card, which made me lose!" Bobby wailed.

Emily paused.

Ten million dollars?

She felt the back of her neck grow incredibly hot.

"Hold on a second. Do you mean to tell me," Emily said dangerously, "that those ghastly rats-with-wings cost us *ten million dollars?*"

Bobby nodded, his eyes flashing ominously in the dimly lit garage.

"Alright. That is *it*. That is the last straw. Hand me that wrench," said Emily determinedly, tying her hair back.

The couple worked into the dead of the night, trying to repair the damage that Emily had inflicted onto the machine. After a few days of continuously working, pouring blood, sweat, and tears into the device, the Pigeon Homing Device was complete. It was a crude device, but they supposed that it had to do.

The machine consisted of a metal box that was hooked to a pair of speakers that emitted the sound of bread crumbs hitting the floor at a sound pitch that only pigeons could hear. It was quite sophisticated, Emily thought as she marvelled at their handiwork. It was a wonder how losing ten million dollars could motivate a person to get their revenge on an entire species.

"Ready?" asked Bobby as he rubbed his hands together in glee. Emily nodded tenaciously. They held in their breaths as Bobby flipped a switch on the metal box. The couple began looking around, listening for the sounds of wings flapping, or the familiar sound of "croo" from the pigeons.

The only sound they could hear was the sound of water dripping from the faucet nearby.

"Well, that was completely anti-climactic."

"Well—" Bobby's response was cut off with a small rumbling sound. They looked about quizzically as the ground beneath them began to thunder precariously.

"Is this an earthquake?" Emily's voice quivered as they ran to find something to take cover underneath for an earthquake.

"I don't know!" Bobby gulped as he braced himself beneath a sturdy table. Emily squeezed herself beside him, getting ready for what the menacing trembling was about to bring upon them. The earth trembled beneath them for what seemed to be days. The couple held on to each other, with Emily's head tucked beneath Bobby's chin and their arms entangled with each other. Once the rumbling had stopped, the couple shakily made their way out from beneath the table.

"Is it safe to go outside?" asked Emily fearfully. Bobby shrugged, clambering over the mess that occurred whilst the earth rumbled beneath them, and peered out of the window. "Oh wow." He breathed.

"How bad is it?" Emily asked as she made her way over to where he was standing.

"You are not going to believe this," Bobby gaped at the sight before them. Outside of their window, a lone pigeon perched on the windowsill, looking quizzically inside the room.

Behind it, a sea of feathered creatures gathered as they chirped at each other in a deafening roar of the familiar "croo."

"I-I can't believe it," Emily gasped as she stared back at the lone pigeon. "It worked. The machine worked!"

The lone pigeon cocked its head to the side and chirped at her before flapping its wings and joining the sea of pigeons behind it, leaving a certain familiar white stain onto the green paint of the windowsill.

"Oh, you have got to be kidding me," Bobby muttered furiously. "They're pooping on my car again!" Sure enough, the pigeons were balanced precariously on a telephone wire that stretched across the road. The ones that were sitting directly above Bobby's car were letting out a continuous stream of bird faeces. Emily watched as it plopped down onto Bobby's car, the red paint no longer visible through the thick layer of droppings that painted the car murky white.

"Well, what do we do now?" asked Emily. Bobby rubbed his neck as he glared at the pigeons murderously.

"We get rid of them all," he said through gritted teeth. "We get rid of them *all*."

"How do you propose we do that?"

Bobby blinked. "That is a good question."

Now it was Emily's turn to glare at him. "You mean to tell me that we spent all that time trying to create a device that would attract pigeons from around the world, and you have absolutely *no idea* how to get rid of them?" she uttered carefully. Bobby nodded hesitantly.

"I can't believe this," Emily said as she threw up her arms in defeat. "What on earth do you think we should do now? We have pigeons covering every inch of our property. We have pigeons around us as far as the eye can see. They are pooping onto our fences, our porch, our *house,* and... oh God," she gasped as she suddenly remembered an important detail.

"We forgot about Splat!" Emily cried in horror as she saw their dog yipping in fear as several pigeons were perched on top of his furry body. A couple of pigeons fluttered their wings in distress as the dog flicked his tail repeatedly in an attempt to get rid of the birds.

"I have to go save Splat!" she cried, thinking of her poor dog miserably covered in pigeon faeces. She moved towards the garage door, but Bobby moved in her way to block her.

"No! I can't let you go outside!" he said as he stretched his arms wide, blocking any access she had to the garage door. "Any sudden movements can send those wretched rats-with-wings into a flying frenzy of manic birds! Who knows what they would do then? It's not worth saving Splat! He never even liked me, anyway!"

"I don't care!" cried Emily. "I have to save Splat!" she barrelled past him and flung the door wide open, calling out for her beloved dog.

Unfortunately, this sent the birds to do exactly what Bobby had predicted.

"No, Emily, no!" Bobby cried out. "You've made a mistake! You've made a mistaaaaaake!" His voice was drowned out by the immediate sound of the deafening roar of flapping wings and pigeons chirping. They looked up to the sky, which had turned into an ominous mottled grey from all the pigeons that were clouding up the sky, effectively blocking out the sun.

"What have you done?" Bobby whispered in a terror-filled gasp. Emily glanced at him, her arms around her dog, her fingers moulding with the matted mess that the birds left in his usually shiny coat. Her eyes clouded over with amazement as she turned her attention back to the cloud of birds that hung threateningly above them. They all seemed to be heading in one direction, like a speckled grey road that split through the sky.

"They're causing an eclipse," Bobby gasped as he watched the pigeons in shock and awe as the cloud of pigeons slowly moved in front of the sun, throwing the world into darkness. "It's the end of the world as we know it."

"Where are they going?" she asked, her voice now sounding very small.

"I don't know," Bobby said as he shook his head. "But let's find out."

The couple raced to the poop-covered car, hastily wiping the door handle clean before hastily getting into the car. Bobby shifted the gears in his car and they took off, following the stream of pigeons that were flying manically, squawking and chirping at each other as they flowed through the atmosphere in waves.

The birds led them to the coast, and they could see the ocean roaring angrily as it began to swallow the pigeons as they began to fly into the water, plunging their bodies into the ice-cold water. The waves around the pigeons began to grow higher and higher, as each of the birds' bodies began to hit the water with such a tremendous force that it disrupted the normally calm water into a raging storm.

"What are they doing?" Emily cried, watching in horror as more and more birds began hurling themselves into the water.

"At this point, I don't care!" said Bobby tiredly. "They're getting rid of themselves for me, and I'm completely wiped out at this point."

"Look, Bobby!"

"No! I just want to go home! I'm tired of this absurd adventure that we're having!" he said stubbornly, completely oblivious to the huge wave that was building up in the water and was headed their way.

"I think we should get as far away from here as possible, NOW," said Emily, grabbing the wheel of the car. "There's a huge tsunami wave heading for us!"

Sure enough, there was a large wave that was headed their way. It washed up right to where the car tires were, and Emily glanced up at the shoreline to see that the ocean had begun to look much more treacherous than when they had first arrived. Everything seemed as if it were playing at high speed. The waves began to grow larger and larger, and began to reach further and further into the mainland.

"Drive, Bobby! DRIVE!" Emily screamed.

With that, Bobby pressed his heel to the gas pedal, and they tore their way out of the coastline and back towards the mainland. Emily turned her head to look behind her and saw that a ginormous wave was tearing its way after them. As the wave began to crash and destroy their surroundings, she could swear that she could hear a faint "croo" in the undertone of the perilous wave.

"I can't believe this," said Bobby, for what seemed to be the hundredth time that day. "Those pesky pigeons are actually *riding* the wave. *They're riding the wave.*"

Sure enough, pigeons could be seen at the crest of the wave, almost as if they were surfing on the perilous wave that would send them to their watery doom. Several pigeons could be seen plunging in and out of the wave, seeming to push it further and faster into the mainland.

"You were right all along, Bobby," Emily said as tears began to well up in her eyes. "Pigeons really *are* the things behind ruining your life. And now they're going to ruin *my* life," she finished with a wail.

Before the wave swallowed their tiny car in its stormy jaws, she heard a definite taunting "croo" sound around her. Her last conscious thought was a string of profanities aimed at the pigeons, and then a last farewell to her beloved Bobby.

And then, there was nothing.

On average, a pigeon has 10,000 feathers on its body.

Epilogue

Bobby blinked, cocking his head to one side as he heard a familiar voice ringing through his ears.

"I'm gonna get you!" a giggly voice called out. He turned around towards the source of the sound. His eyes widened in alarm as a large stick was heading straight towards him. He jumped quickly out of the way, sighing in relief as he watched the stick sail past him. "I said, I'm gonna GET YOU!" the voice said again. This time, the stick prodded him in the chest. He frowned, annoyed at the stick. He looked up to see a toddler's face peering closely at him, grinning gleefully.

Oh, great. A child. Bobby hated children.

He jerked in alarm when he felt something being pulled from his bottom. The toddler's hand emerged with several feathers in his fist. Where was he getting those feathers from? Bobby glared at the toddler.

"Bobby! Leave that poor bird alone!"

Bobby snapped his head towards the other voice. It all seemed so familiar. He hadn't heard that voice in years…

It couldn't be, could it?

He was looking up at his big sister, Sally. She looked much younger from when he last saw her. She was standing at the doorway to his childhood home, with her hands resting on her hips as she began to berate the small child about kindness to animals.

The toddler…

Bobby looked up to see his five-year old self's face peering at him curiously.

How was this possible?

He flapped his wings, almost doing a double take as he realized how easy it was for him to simply float off of the ground.

He perched himself on a branch next to his house, watching as his younger self grumpily rested his head on his hand, looking quite bored. His curiosity peaked, and he hopped closer to the window, tapping his beak onto the glass. He smiled to himself as he watched little Bobby clamber towards the window in excitement, pushing the glass open.

Bobby slipped inside. It was all too bizarre.

Suddenly, he flapped his wings in alarm as he felt a hand close over his small, delicate body. A slow, oozing liquid dripped down his back, and he felt a small shower of small objects land onto his back.

This all seemed far too familiar.

Oh no.

Little Bobby was covering him in glue and glitter.

That was it. He was out. There was no way he was going to let himself be degraded and covered in a sticky, glittery mess.

"Where are you going, Pigeon? You forgot your eyes!"

Bobby froze as he heard little Bobby. Whatever did he mean? Was he going to pull out his eyes?

His question was answered as he felt some more oozing liquid, and another short shower of objects on his back.

The googly-eyes. How could he forget?

Bobby was just about to escape when he felt some pressure on his head. Oh yes, the antennas.

"Now you look so pretty!" Little Bobby chirped. Bobby turned around to examine himself in the mirror.

He was anything *but* pretty.

And he hated being called pretty, anyway. "Croo."

Bobby glared at his toddler self before grinning evilly to himself.

He had the perfect revenge. With a little pressure, he relieved himself onto the table and hopped away, watching as Little Bobby examined the small, white patch that he had left behind.

"Croo," he called as he flapped his way back outside.

He made a full circle around the house, trying to rid himself of the gluey mess on his body.

Unfortunately, the feathers got even more matted and messy. Oh yes, he definitely needed his revenge.

Bobby flew back towards his house, searching for an open window. Finally spotting one, he landed outside, peering into what he recognized was the bathroom.

He scratched at the window with his foot, trying to get the person's attention inside.

It was Little Bobby, who was playing with his little toy airplane in the bath. Little Bobby smiled delightedly as he saw him outside.

"Pigeon! So you *do* remember me!" he cried happily. Bobby chuckled to himself, landing on the toddler's head and digging his claws into his hair, relieving himself once more.

He could get used to this.

Afterword

I've always been fascinated with pigeons. I remember when I was eight-years-old on a family vacation, and I was waiting for a bus with my dad. At the bus station, among the continuous throngs of people moving in and out, was a smaller community that lived on an entirely different level.

Literally speaking. This community lived quite close to the ground.

This community was made up of pigeons, of course.

I remember wanting to run up to a particular pigeon that had wandered too close to me. Its feathers around its neck was shimmering between a deep purple and turquoise, and being a curious, mischievous eight-year-old child, I wanted nothing more than to run up to that shiny pigeon bobbing its little head back and forth and examining a few stray crumbs lying on the floor before pecking at it.

My dad, being the responsible parent that he was, stopped me from running towards the pigeon and petting it, telling me that it was unsanitary and that I could get sick from touching it.

Needless to say, I was quite disappointed.

As I grew up, my fascination with pigeons began to grow as well. I was mainly unaware of my interest in those creatures, which usually came as an afterthought or a comment in the middle of a conversation that I would be having with someone. One would catch my eye, and I would begin narrating its supposed life story, and how it got there, and what was it doing.

My encounters with pigeons were always stricken with humorous events. In the mornings, there was always a flock of pigeons congregating outside of my house in the middle of the road. Those pigeons seemed to have a sense of authority, and refused to move off of the road. Anyone who happened to be driving by always had to slow down their car and honk so that the pigeons would finally fly away, leaving the driver with a safe passage.

And every now and then, a car would get hit with a splatter of pigeon poop.

People always seemed to be annoyed with pigeons, yet I always found situations with pigeons to be quite funny. "Rats-with-wings," some of my friends would comment as one would strut by us, bobbing its tiny head as it passed by.

I began making up little stories about pigeons so much to the point where someone told me, "Why don't you just write a book about them?"

In hindsight, it was probably more out of exasperation than encouragement.

Nonetheless, I took the advice and began to compile my pigeon stories.

Bobby was an especially amusing character to invent and write out. In a lot of ways, young Bobby seems to resemble the way that I used to interact with animals when I was a child. My friends confirmed this when I described

Bobby to them, and they laughed at his little mannerisms that seemed to reflect my own.

Throughout the entire time that I had been writing *The Pigeon Chronicles,* my friends and family have been asking me why I chose to write such a bizarre book after the first one had been so serious. To be entirely honest, I think that this type of story is a more accurate representation of what my writing style is like. I also had a lot of fun writing these stories, which was the very motivation that I needed in order to write out such peculiar stories.

Special Thanks

I would love to take the time to thank my friends and family who willingly took the time to listen to my ramblings about pigeons and their stories, and supported my idea to create *The Pigeon Chronicles*.